This book belongs to:

....

....

....

yum yum

A TEMPLAR BOOK

First Published in the UK in 2019 by Templar Books,

an imprint of Bonnier Books UK

4th Floor, Victoria House,

Bloomsbury Square, London WC1B 4DA

Owned by Bonnier Books

Sveavägen 56, Stockholm, Sweden

www.bonnierbooks.co.uk

Copyright © Anna Llenas, 2018

First published in Spain by by Editorial Flamboyant S.L. in 2018

under the title EL MONSTRE DE COLORS VA A L'ESCOLA

10 9

ISBN 978-1-78741-5522 (Paperback)

ISBN 978-1-78741-558-4 (Hardback)

This book was typeset in Meta

The illustrations were created with acrylic and collage

Printed in China

The Colour Monster goes to SCHOOL

ANNA LLENAS

templar
books

Hello, Colour Monster!

Guess what?

Today is your first day of school.

School? What *is* that?

Is it a spooky castle
filled with monsters and beasts?

Is it up in the sky with
rainbows and clouds?

Is it in a scary jungle guarded
by evil plants?

Here's your rucksack, Colour Monster.
What do you think you'll need?

Helmet

Boots
(for quicksand)

**Alien-spotting
goggles**

**Bat
repellent**

Torch

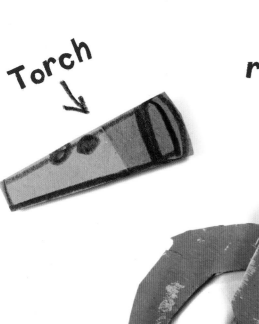

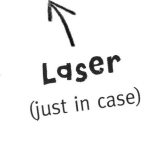

Laser
(just in case)

What are you going to do with all this stuff?
You just need your coat and a notebook!

Here we are! This is our school.
I promise we're going to have a great day.

Goodbye, kids!

Hello, Ms Edwards!
This is my friend the Colour Monster.
It's his first day of school!

First we need to go to
our classroom.

Where are you hiding?

Why don't you come out and meet your classmates? Don't be scared!
Their names are:

Nuna

Lucas

Tortie

Max

Martin

Valentín

Leo

Lucy

Chloe

Yun

Our first lesson this morning is music. That's my favourite class!

You're doing great! You're just a little bit out of tune . . .

Then Ms Edwards reads us a story.

You seem to *really* like stories, Colour Monster!

Later, we go to the playground.

Hey, Colour Monster . . . Can we *please* have a turn on the swing?

Before lunch,
we go to the toilet
and wash our hands.

Splish
splosh

What are you doing,
Colour Monster?

No! Don't do that!

I'm really hungry now! At last it's time for lunch.

Look Colour Monster, today we're having bread and soup!

Nooo – it's hot!

You shouldn't play with
your food!

In the afternoon, we go to the gym to do some exercise.

Jumping on the Colour Monster is so much fun!

We end the day by doing some painting.

We've got the best model –
the Colour Monster can change colour!

Don't blink,
he might
turn pink!

When school is over, it's time to say goodbye.

What a fun day!

Bye, Ms Edwards!

See you tomorrow!

I knew you'd have a good day!

School isn't so bad after all, is it?

But now I need to nap . . . I'm *exhausted*!

Draw the Colour Monster here:

Anna Llenas used to love going to school to learn – of course! – but also to draw. Later on, she became a graphic designer and worked in advertising. One day she decided that she wanted to make beautiful drawings again and she left everything to dedicate herself to the publishing world. Today, she is the well-known author of many books; among them, international bestseller *The Colour Monster*.

www.annallenas.com

For more Colour Monster adventures:

The Colour Monster
ISBN: 978-1-78370-423-1 (Paperback)
ISBN: 978-1-78741-273-6 (Board book)

The Colour Monster:
A Colour Activity Book
ISBN: 978-1-78370-459-0